THIS BOOK
BELONGS TO

· · · · · · · · · · · · · · ·
· · · · · · · · · · · · · · · ·

For my mother, Margaret

Copyright © 2008
by Charlotte Voake
Based on the traditional folk
song "The Green Leaves Grew Around,"
which has no known writer or
copyright holder.

First U.S. edition 2008

Library of Congress Cataloging-in-Publication Data is available
Library of Congress Catalog Card Number pending

ISBN 978-07636-3797-2

10 9 8 7 6 5 4 3 2 1

Printed in China

This book was typeset in Charlotte.
The illustrations were done
in watercolor and ink.

Candlewick Press
2067 Massachusetts Avenue
Cambridge, Massachusetts 02140

visit us at www.candlewick.com

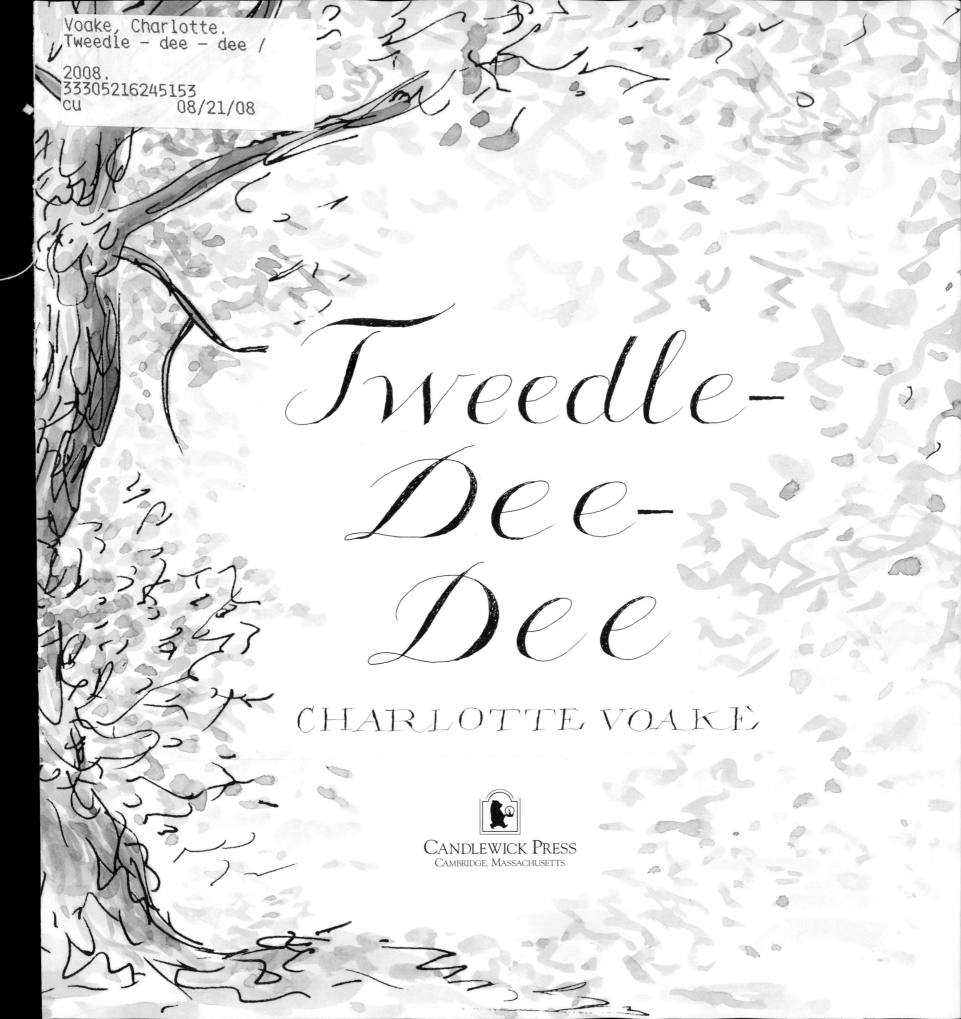

Tweedle-Dee-Dee

CHARLOTTE VOAKE

CANDLEWICK PRESS
CAMBRIDGE, MASSACHUSETTS

ONCE in a wood
there was
a tree,

the finest tree
you ever did
see.

And the green
leaves grew
around, around,
around,

and the green leaves
grew around.

AND
on that tree
there was
a branch,
the finest branch
you ever
did see.

AND on that branch there was a nest, the finest nest you ever did see.

The branch was
on the tree,
the tree was in
the wood,
and the green
leaves grew
around,
around, around,
and the green leaves
grew around.

The nest was on
the branch,

the branch was on
the tree,

the tree was in
the wood,

and the green
leaves grew around,
around, around,

and the green leaves
grew around.

ANd in
that nest there
were some eggs,
the finest little
eggs you ever
did see.

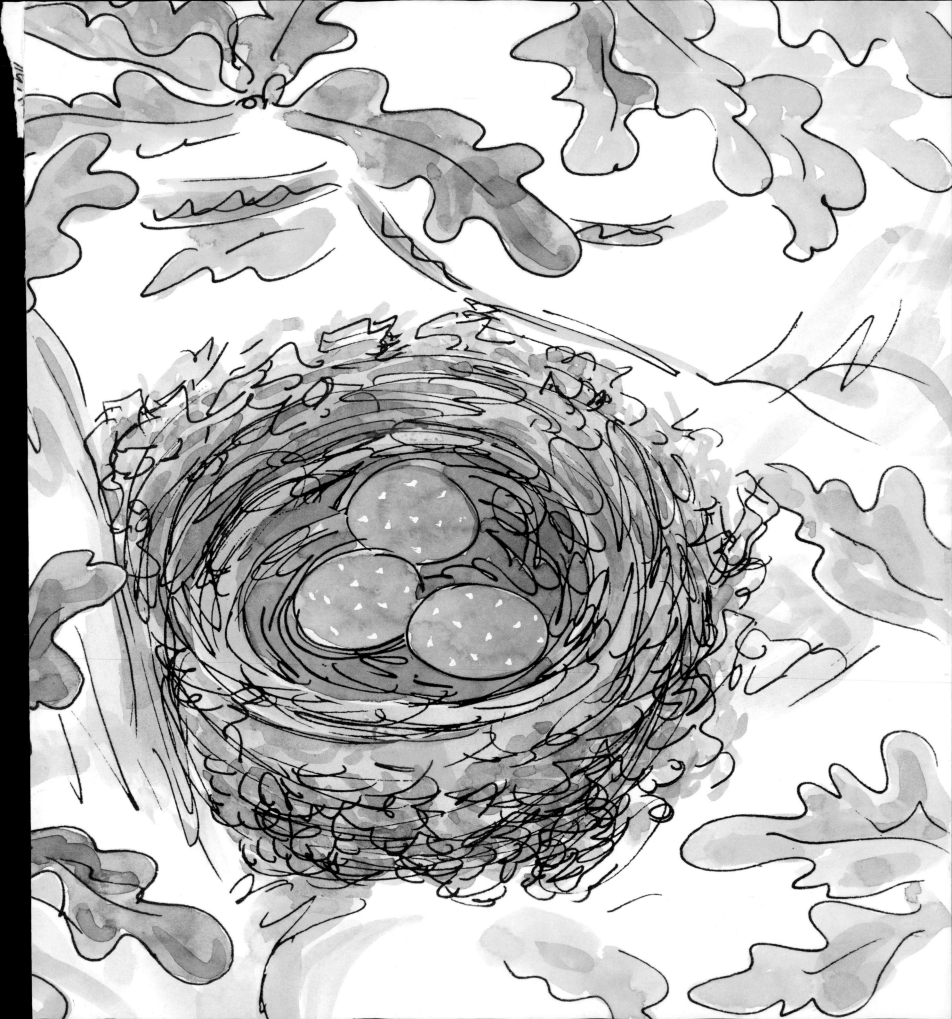

The eggs were
in the nest,

the nest was
on the branch,

the branch
was on the tree,

the tree was in
the wood,

and the green leaves
grew around, around,
around, and the green
leaves grew around.

AND in those eggs there were some birds,

ONE and TWO and THREE!

"CHEEP!" went one,
"CHEEP!" went another,
and the third went,

"TWEEDLE-
DEE-DEE!"

The birds were in
the eggs,

the eggs were in
the nest,

the nest was on
the branch,

the branch was
on the tree,

the tree was
in the wood...

and the green leaves grew
around, around, around,
and the birds went,

"TWEEDLE-
DEE-DEE!"

THE TREE SONG